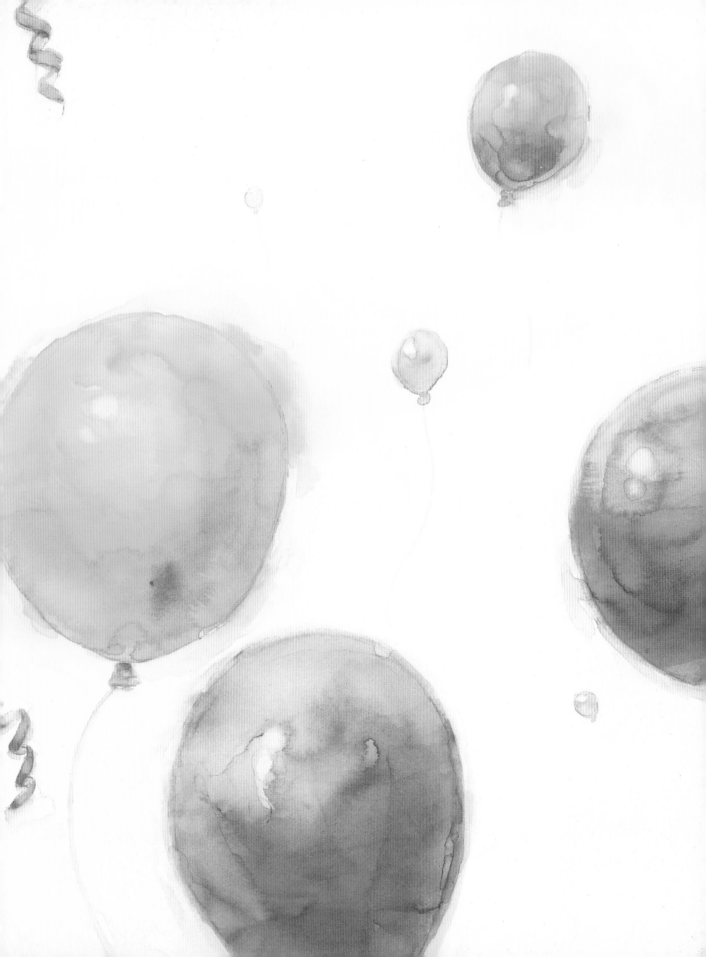

Dedicated to the children of East Harlem and barrios everywhere. — M.S.

For Deborah, an original. — Y.H. & C.V.W.

Este libro está dedicado a los niños de East Harlem y de todos los otros barrios. — M.S.

Para Deborah, alguien verdaderamente original. —Y.H. & C.V.W.

Published in the US by Star Bright Books, Inc.
The name Star Bright Books and the Star Bright Books logo are
registered trademarks of Star Bright Books, Inc.

Please visit: www.starbrightbooks.com. For orders,
email: orders@starbrightbooks.com or call: (617) 354-1300.

Spanish/English Hardcover ISBN: 978-1-59572-115-0
Star Bright Books / MA / 00307080
Printed in China / WKT / 10 9 8 7 6 5 4 3

Spanish/English Paperback ISBN: 978-1-59572-116-7
Star Bright Books / MA / 00605210
Printed in China / WKT / 10 9 8 7 6

Printed on paper from sustainable forest.

Library of Congress Cataloging-in-Publication Data

Starr, Meg.
    [Alicia's happy day. English & Spanish]
    Alicia's happy day / by Meg Starr ; illustrated by Ying-hwa Hu & Cornelius Van Wright ; translated by
Maria Fiol. El dia mas feliz de Alicia / por Meg Starr ; ilustrado por Ying-hwa Hu & Cornelius Van
Wright ; traducido por Maria Fiol.
          p. cm.
    Summary: Alicia receives greetings from her Hispanic neighborhood as she walks to her birthday party.
    ISBN-13: 978-1-59572-116-7 (pbk.)
    ISBN-10: 1-59572-116-9 (pbk.)
    [1. Birthdays--Fiction. 2. Parties--fiction. 3. Hispanic America--Fiction. 4. Spanish language
material--Bilingual.] I. Hu, Ying-hwa, ill. II. Van Wright, Cornelius, ill. III. Fiol, Maria A. IV. Title.
V. Title: Dia mas Feliz de Alicia.

PZ73.S7515 2006
[E]-dc22

                              2006035223

ALICIA'S HAPPY DAY
EL DÍA MÁS FELIZ DE ALICIA

By/Por Meg Starr

Illustrated by/Ilustrado por
Ying-hwa Hu & Cornelius Van Wright
Translated by/Traducido por María Fiol

STAR BRIGHT BOOKS
CAMBRIDGE MASSACHUSETTS

May you have a day
that's twirly-swirly.

¡Ojalá que pases un
día muy feliz!

May you hear salsa and start to dance.

Que oigas salsa y empieces a bailar.

May the flags
all fly for you.

Que todas las
banderas ondeen
en tu honor.

Taxicabs all stop for you.

Que todos los taxis
se detengan para ti.

Airplanes write in
the sky for you.

Que los aviones escriban
en el cielo para ti.

Walk signs say "Walk"
in time for you,

Que las señales
de tráfico indiquen
"Camina" justo
cuando llegues.

And pigeons bow
shiny necks to you.

Que las palomas se
inclinen para saludarte.

While friends
decorate in
chalk for you.

Que tus amigos
hagan dibujos con
tiza para ti.

May the Orange lady give
a ribbon of peel to you,

Que la vendedora de naranjas te regale
una cinta de cáscara de naranja.

And the Icey man say,
"Helado de Coco for you."

Que el
heladero diga:
"¡Un helado de
coco para ti!".

May Mommy and Daddy hug you,

Que papi y mami
te abracen.

Auntie Penelope
sing to you,

Que Titi Penélope
cante para ti.

Baby Anibal give
his bobo to you.

Que el bebé Aníbal
te dé su chupete.

May you laugh as loud as you want with no one to stop you, because all of us, we're all for you—that's why we sing happy birthday to YOU!

Que rías con todas tus ganas sin que nadie te interrumpa, porque todos nosotros te queremos y por eso te cantamos: "¡Cumpleaños feliz te deseamos a TI!".